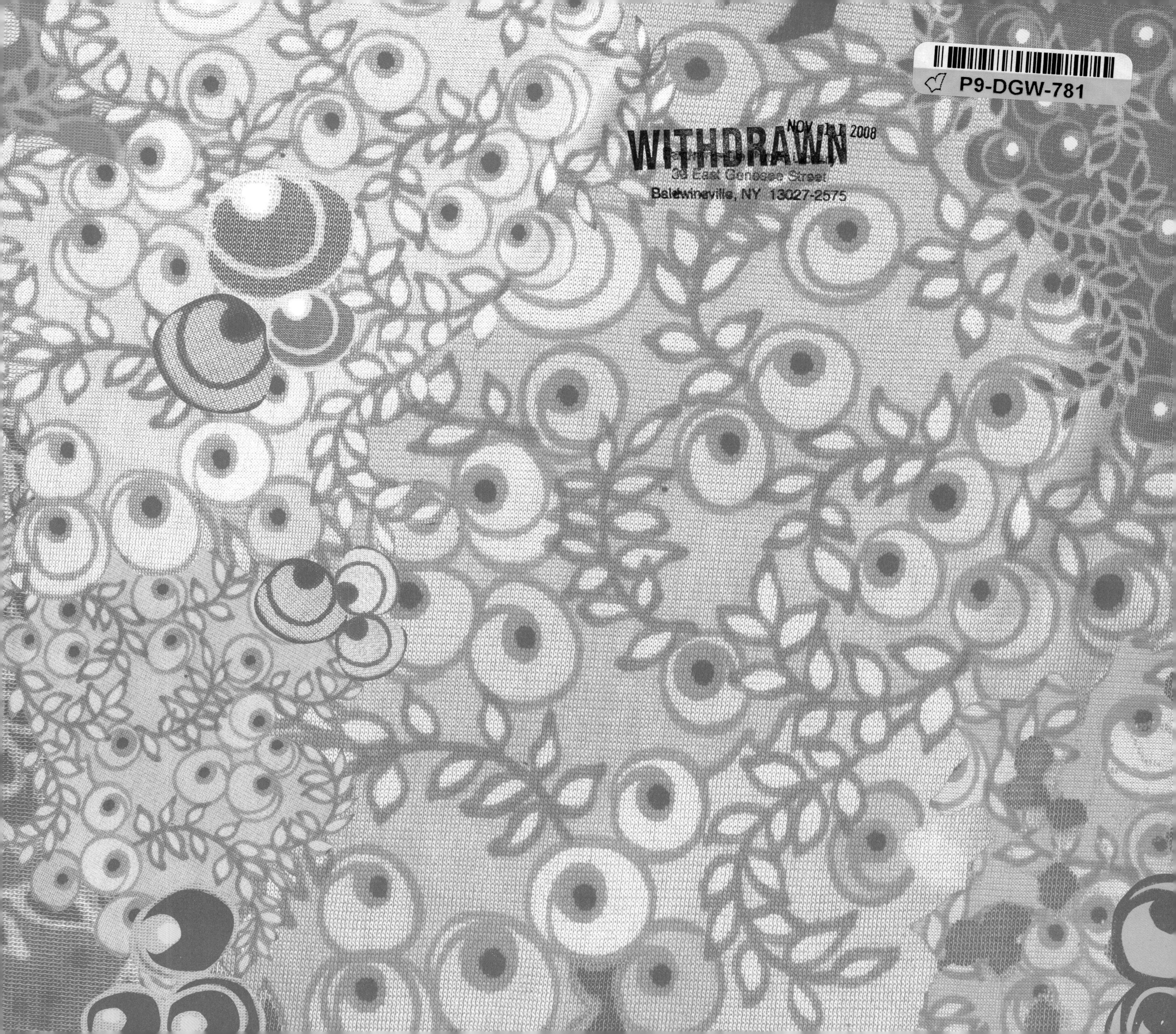

BORIS
and the
Snoozebox

Name: ....

Address: ....

....

....

For
Cleo

(who is probably too
busy being asleep
to read this book)

& Mr. Steve Smith
(who occasionally
wishes he was a cat)

tiger tales

an imprint of ME Media, LLC

202 Old Ridgefield Road, Wilton, CT 06897

Published in the United States 2008

Originally published in Great Britain 2007

by Orchard Books

Orchard Books is a division of Hachette Children's Books,

an Hachette Livre UK company

Text and illustrations copyright © 2007 Leigh Hodgkinson

CIP data is available

ISBN-13: 978-1-58925-071-0

ISBN-10: 1-58925-071-0

Printed in China NOV 1 1 2008

O
P
Q
R
S
T
U
V
W
X
Y
Z

BORIS

and the
Snoozebox

MEOW MAIL 0103
POSTAGE PAID
50509699

by Leigh
Hodgkinson

tiger tales

scampering,

licking,

BALANCING,

and looking cute.

However . . .

it is **NOT** OK

when he is tired, *GROUCHY*, and in desperate need of a long catnap.

At times like this, Boris would do anything for

a plumpish pillow to snuggle onto.

ANYTHING.
(Even give up singing...maybe.)

As Boris sleepily snoops and sniffs around, he spies a **boring** old…

Everything

CARDBOARD BOX.

Boring maybe …
but if you look inside,
it is completely perfect for
dozing and snooooooooooo …

oooooooooooooozing.

Boris dreams that his ears are being TICKLED.

Boris dreams about a big fish.
(This is his favorite dream, by the way.)

JOLT

THUNK

SHUFFLE

SHUFFLE

FRAGILE

This box,

of all
boxes,
is a

real mover

and SHAKER.

What on EARTH is going on?

THIS END UP

Lady Snootlethorpe is **delighted** that her package has arrived.

At last, the BIGGEST teapot in the world will be hers....

Lady Snootlethorpe gets quite
a surprise when she opens the box.

(So does poor Boris.)

FRAGILE

"This is **NOT** what I ordered!" she shrieks.
"*I* **DON'T** want this cat, and it must be sent back!"

Lid down. ↓   Taped up. ↑   The box is zoomed off,
all the way to . . .

Mr. Marshmallow, who is a pretty picky eater.
He will only eat fish from the South Pole
(which is RIDICULOUS because he lives on the other one).

So,

Mr. Marshmallow gets his fish delivered right to his ice block.

The timing of today's delivery couldn't be more perfect.

URGENT

Grandma FLAPJACK'S house (Not here!)

His freezer is empty and he is HUGELY HUNGRY.

It has to be said that Mr. Marshmallow is a smidgen disappointed.

"Absolutely NO fish in here, just a silly cat," Mr. Marshmallow mutters miserably.

Boris is already aware of this piece of information.

(Well, apart from the bit about him being silly, which is news to him.)

Boris wishes
there were oodles
of fish in the box with him.

He, too, is hungry
and could use a nibble on
something tasty.

Uh-oh!

It looks as though Boris
is on the move again....

"This is the **wrong** package. This is a MISTAKE! There has been major mix-up. I didn't order a pet. I have one already!"

Mister Gobbledeegook jabbers

ANGRILY.

(He has been waiting light-years for his remote-controlled space butterfly.)

Boris wonders

if he is the first cat in space.

Boris wonders if he is finally asleep,

and if he has fallen into his own dream.

Boris wonders where he is going next....

Every single time, it is **exactly** the same.
To be honest, Boris is beginning to get slightly **BORED** of it.
Every time he drifts off to sleep,

someone opens the box and wakes him **up!**

Beady eyes peek inside...

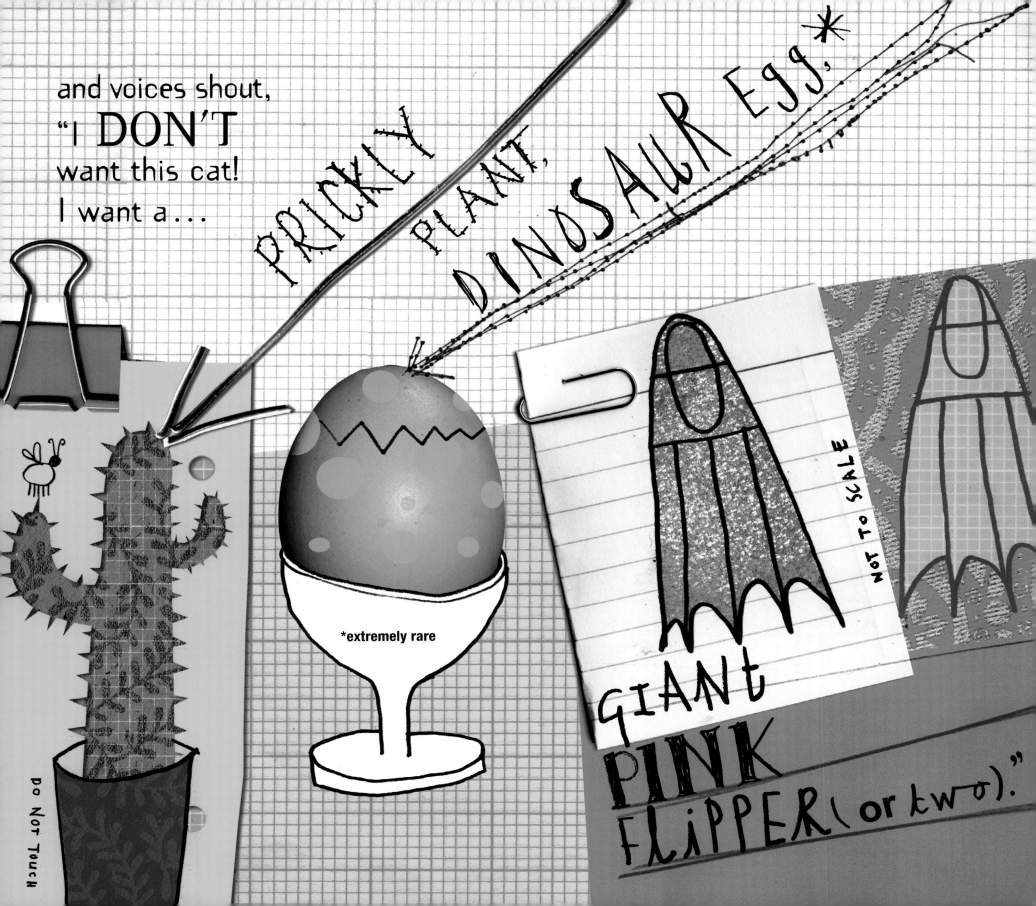

POOR OLD BORIS.

All he wants is a little peace and quiet.
All he wants is at least forty or so winks
in his homemade hideout with
NO trouble **whatsoever.**
Is that REALLY too much to ask?

Yet he **keeps** being interrupted by
rude MEANIES, ONLY to be told that
they wish he wasn't there.

And nobody
—nobody—
likes to hear that.

Boris decides he has HAD

ENOUGH

and comes up with a plan.
He will try extra-specially hard
to stay awake, and the next
chance he gets, he will

JUMP

out of the box
and make a

r u n for it.

Meanwhile,
not so far away from Boris ...

Grandma Flapjack isn't expecting a delivery at all.

Grandma Flapjack's house
(Yes YES! Here Please!)

THIS END UP

WELCOME

For some reason, she never ever gets **anything** interesting in the mail.
Yet there seems to be a rather LARGE package outside her door right now.

Maybe there has been a mistake**?**

As she opens the mysterious box, a super-sour puss leaps out and lands on ...

the world's most comfy pillow.

DO NOT BE
URGENT
FR
AIRMAIL
URGENT

Boris looks up and sees a **friendly** face. This is a pleasant change!

"I have always wanted a cat!" says Grandma Flapjack.
This is funny, as Boris has always wanted a Grandma Flapjack.

(He just didn't know her name.)

She pets him,

brushes him,

feeds him,

AND plunks the purring pampered puss back on his pillow.

With a plumpish belly and two ears fully **tickled**, Boris is feeling oh-so snugglishly

cozy

in his new home.

In situations like this, there is only one thing to do. . . .

Boris

yawns

and decides that perhaps it's about time for a little catnap.

do not <u>not</u> disturb

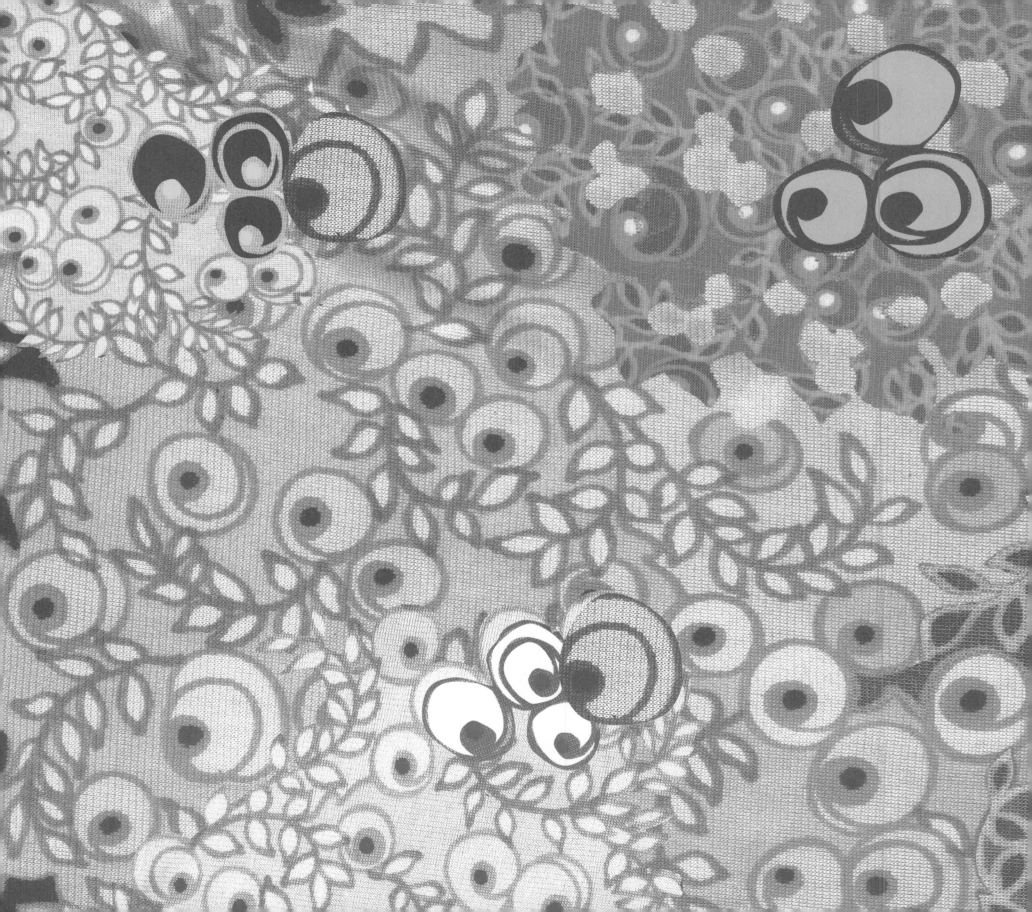